Stephen Coxhead

Ronnie Rhino
and the
MISSING HORN

Limited Special Edition. No. 19 of 25 Paperbacks

Stephen was born and brought up in Yateley, Hampshire. He
is a qualified accountant and has been chief financial officer of
a variety of businesses. He enjoys sport, is a qualified hockey
coach and enjoys watching his three children develop their love
of sport, while writing children's stories to read to them in his
spare time. He is also passionate about raising awareness of the
plight of animals that are endangered, hence the
theme of his books.

Hope you enjoy

Stephen Coxhead

Ronnie Rhino
and the
MISSING HORN

AUSTIN MACAULEY PUBLISHERS™
LONDON • CAMBRIDGE • NEW YORK • SHARJAH

A CIP catalogue record for this title is available from the British Library.

ISBN 9781528920049 (Paperback)
ISBN 9781528962964 (ePub e-book)

www.austinmacauley.com

First Published (2020)
Austin Macauley Publishers Ltd
25 Canada Square
Canary Wharf
London
E14 5LQ

To my nan that ploughed the fields
My mum and dad who sowed the seeds
They brought me up and encouraged me
While attending to my needs
To my wife, Janine, who married me
And gave me three great kids
Callum, Liam and Lucy
I love them all to bits.

Ronnie is a rhino calf, he loves to run and play
He scampers through the grassland having fun the
rhino way.
He rolls in mud and eats some grass and rubs
against a tree
And when his friends play kiss chase, he has to try
and flee.

One day, when he went out to play,
his mum said, "Don't stay late
Don't let the sun go down on you,
it really won't be great.

I heard there could be
poachers in the grassland
or the bush
So staying out past 5
o'clock, really is a push."

Ronnie was having so much fun, he lost track of the time
When he looked up at the sun, he thought it could be nine.

He went back home, galloping as
fast has he could run
But on the ground, when he got
home, he saw his poorly mum.

His mum was hurt, she said that poachers hurt her with a gun
She said that she would be OK but that he had to run.
He just did not know what to do, he was really torn
It's then he saw the poachers had taken off her horn.

He ran and ran to find his
friend called Rock,
the Crocodile
He said that he may have to
stay with him for a while.
Rock said, "Why are you sad and looking so forlorn?"
Ronnie replied, "My mum's been hurt and she has
lost her horn."

"Well, come with me," he said, "we will
have to go and take a look
We'll go and ask our jungle
friends, down beside
the brook."
Harvey Hippopotamus
was wading in the mud
He stood up and climbed out of
the river with a thud.

Harvey
said, "Why
are you sad
and looking so forlorn?"
Ronnie replied, "My mum's been hurt
and   she has lost   her horn."

"Well
worry not, my
trusted friend, for
I will spread the word.
I'll tell Annie Antelope and she'll
tell it to the herd."

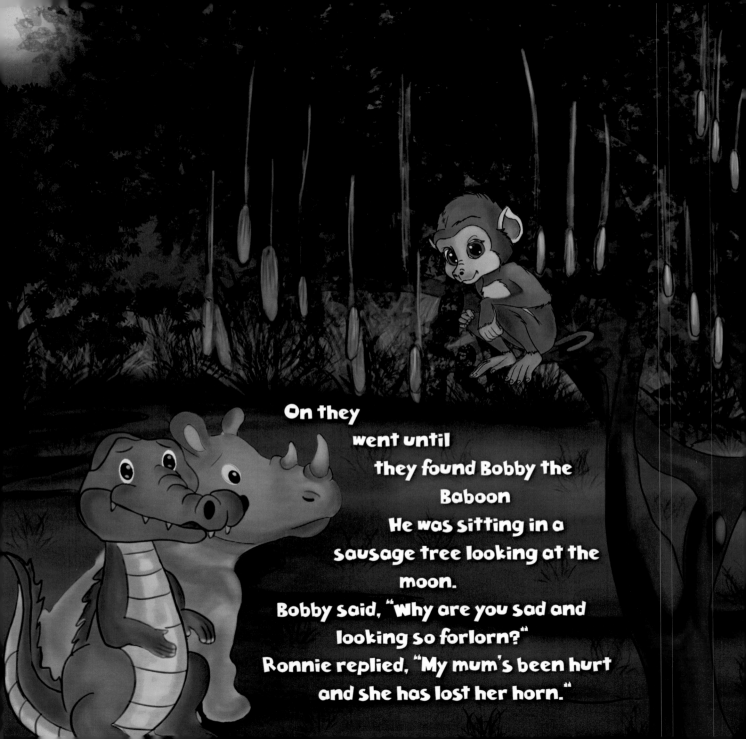

On they went until they found Bobby the Baboon
He was sitting in a sausage tree looking at the moon.
Bobby said, "Why are you sad and looking so forlorn?"
Ronnie replied, "My mum's been hurt and she has lost her horn."

"Leave it to me," Bobby replied, "for I will swing around
To every tree in the land until her horn is found."
On they went until they came across some Wildebeest
Their noses pointed to the ground as they enjoyed their feast.

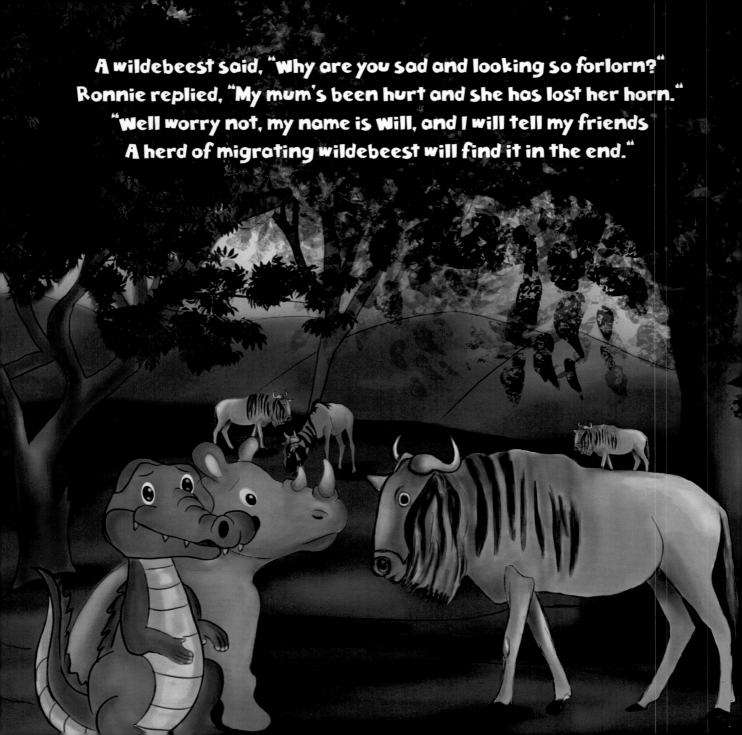

A wildebeest said, "Why are you sad and looking so forlorn?"
Ronnie replied, "My mum's been hurt and she has lost her horn."
"Well worry not, my name is Will, and I will tell my friends
A herd of migrating wildebeest will find it in the end."

Just then, Minnie Myna
Bird fluttered down onto
the ground
And when she opened
up her beak, she made a
pretty sound.
Minnie said, "Why are you
sad and looking
so forlorn?"

Ronnie replied, "My mum's been
hurt and she has lost her horn."

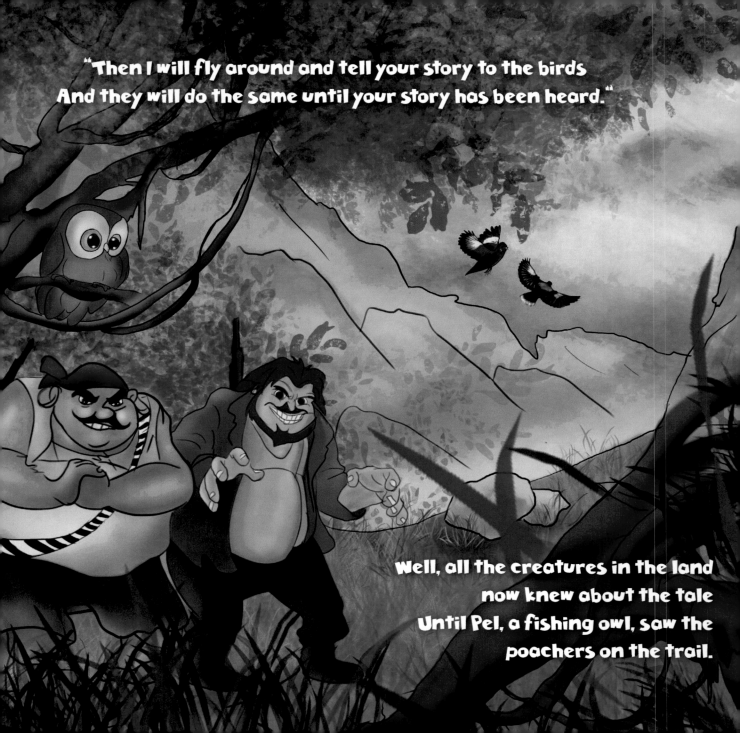

"Then I will fly around and tell your story to the birds
And they will do the same until your story has been heard."

Well, all the creatures in the land
now knew about the tale
Until Pel, a fishing owl, saw the
poachers on the trail.

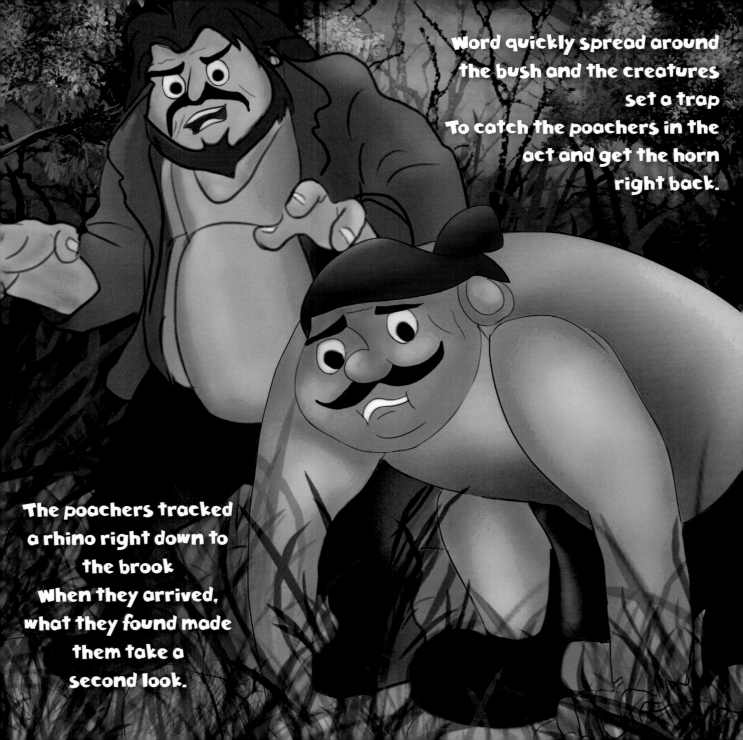

Word quickly spread around
the bush and the creatures
set a trap
To catch the poachers in the
act and get the horn
right back.

The poachers tracked
a rhino right down to
the brook
When they arrived,
what they found made
them take a
second look.

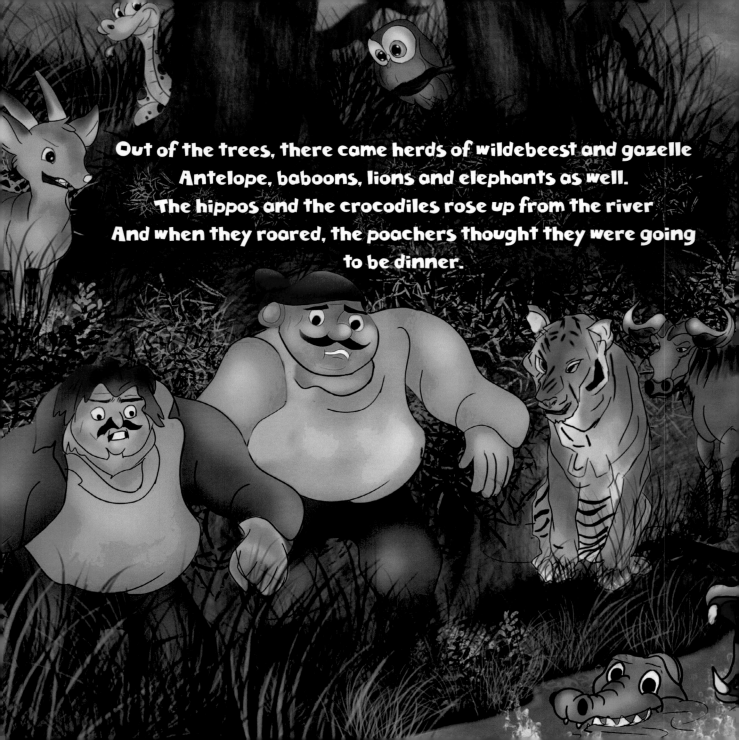

Out of the trees, there came herds of wildebeest and gazelle
Antelope, baboons, lions and elephants as well.
The hippos and the crocodiles rose up from the river
And when they roared, the poachers thought they were going
to be dinner.

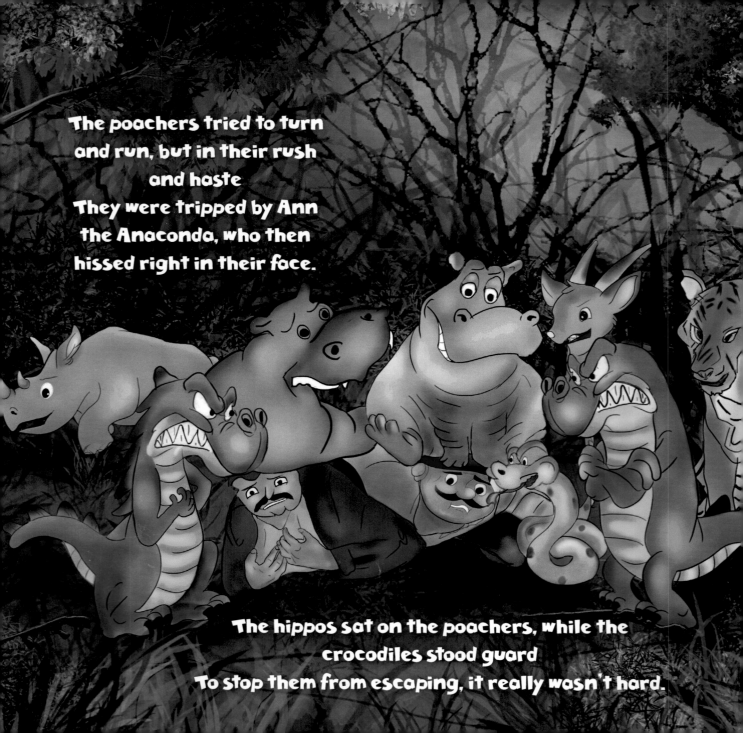

The poachers tried to turn
and run, but in their rush
and haste
They were tripped by Ann
the Anaconda, who then
hissed right in their face.

The hippos sat on the poachers, while the
crocodiles stood guard
To stop them from escaping, it really wasn't hard.

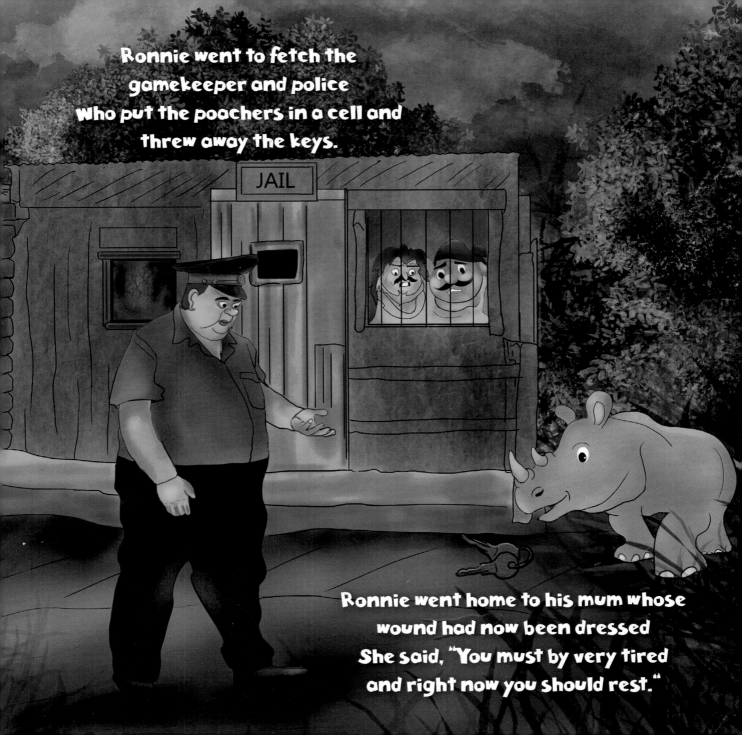

Ronnie went to fetch the
gamekeeper and police
Who put the poachers in a cell and
threw away the keys.

Ronnie went home to his mum whose
wound had now been dressed
She said, "You must by very tired
and right now you should rest."

He told his mum that he was sorry that her horn could not be found
He thought they could have sold it or it may have fallen on the ground.
She said "Ronnie, you are very brave and the horn for now, could keep
But now you need to go to bed and catch up on your sleep."

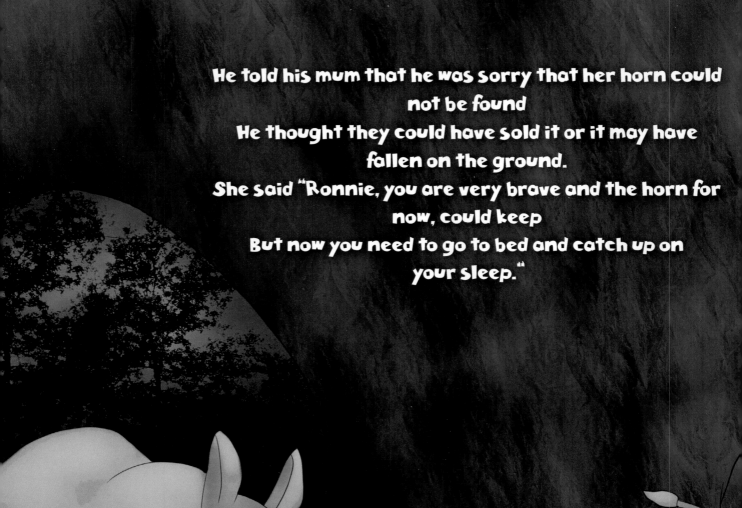